WITHDRAWN

Matilda's HUMDINGER

story by Lynn Downey

illustrations by Tim Bowers

Alfred A. Knopf New York

$\mathcal{M}$atilda worked at Burt's Diner on the corner of Fifth and Main. But her mind was usually somewhere else: duelin' pirates, lassoin' bad guys, or wrestlin' twisters with one hand tied behind her back.

On account of her being so wrapped up in her stories, Matilda was plumb near the worst waitress the diner'd ever seen. She was forever comin' in late, mixin' up orders, and bumpin' into tables. And *that* was on her good days.

Long ago she explained, "Ideas come flyin' at me like a freight train. I figure either I jump on and go where they take me or just stay put and watch 'em pass me by. But," she added proudly, "I ain't never missed one yet."

Folks loved to guess what kind of story Matilda had brewin'.
When she fluttered about all googly-eyed, hummin' a little ditty,
they knew she must be conjurin' up a romance. If they caught
her prowlin' around corners and sneakin' behind chairs, by golly,
she had a mystery spinnin'. And if she greeted a body by slappin'
'em on the back and howlin', "Howdy, pardner! Can I rustle ya up
some grub?"—sure as shootin', everybody knew it was a Western.

Word would spread like wildfire around town that Matilda was at it again, and the diner'd be packed tighter than a jar of dill pickles. Then Matilda would plant herself on the counter like a potted petunia and begin.

"AAAAAAA!! There's a rattler in yer pants!" she shrieked at the beginning of one story, scarin' the bejeebers outta everybody. Big Willy was so shook up, it took three firefighters to coax him down from the ceiling.

Savin' for that, Matilda had a way of keepin'
everybody right glued to their seats, itchin' to
find out what happened next.

"Come on back tomorrow and find out," she'd
say. And everybody did.

So that's how it went. Burt's business boomed,
Matilda made messes and told stories, and
everybody was happy.

That is, until the day a fella by the name of Mr. Ralph Q.
Yuckley moseyed in.

Matilda was smack-dab in the middle of a story when a
loud "tsk, tsk, tsk" came from the back of the room. Folks
started turnin' round to see who on the face of God's green
earth would be tsk, tsk, tskin' at Matilda's story. Finally,
Matilda stopped reading, fixin' both fists on her hips. The
crowd parted and she was face to face with . . . a city slicker.

"You gotta problem, mister—or are you just suckin' at
something stuck between your teeth?" Matilda asked.

His face turned chili-pepper red. "Well! Excuse me for interruptin' your story time, Miss Snooty Patootie—but I thought this was a diner, not a kindygarten."

"Just one cotton-pickin' minute!" Burt cried. "Who do you think you are?"

"*I* am Mr. Ralph Q. Yuckley, U.S. Government Health Inspector. And I am officially citin' this place—*and you, missy*—for violatin' over thirty health codes." He unfolded a mile-long list.

Violations
1. Failure to wear a hairnet.
2. Sitting on a counter where food is served.
3. Dirty dishes on the tables.
4. Spilled milk on the floor.
5. Nametag—upside down.
6. No entertainment license.

"Now!" said Yuckley. "You have two weeks to make this place a proper food-service organization or I'll shut you down faster than a ghost says boo! Do I make myself clear?"

Burt nodded. But for the first time, Matilda was speechless.

After he left, Matilda set to work straightenin' her name tag and puttin' on a hairnet. She spent days cleanin' and scrubbin' till everything in the diner sparkled. Everything, that is, except Matilda. And Burt had a hunch why.

"Maybe you could write some of your stories down at home," he offered.

"Maybe so," Matilda sighed, but she was plumb tuckered out.

Matilda learned to be polite and respectful, neat and tidy. She learned the proper way to serve and how to walk graceful-like. But all that learnin' took a lot of concentration—so much that Matilda had nothin' left over for stories. The diner just wasn't the same. Everybody missed the old Matilda.

Two weeks to the day later, Matilda spotted Ralph Q. Yuckley swaggering up to the door. Suddenly a dreamy look came over her eyes. Her lips turned up in a smile as she pictured him in a ten-gallon hat and sheriff's badge.

Now, Burt could almost smell the engines burnin' in that head of hers, so he hurried her off to the back room, where Matilda began writin' fast and furious. Before she knew it, she'd finished a whole chapter of a Western called *Gone with the Blazes.* She just had to hear how it sounded, so she started reading out loud.

Meanwhile, up front, two strangers burst into the diner.

"This is a stickup!" one grumbled. "Fork over yer loot!"

"You too, pip-squeak!" the other barked at Ralph Q. Yuckley.

"Y-yes, s-sir," he replied, emptyin' his pockets and then divin' under a table, his teeth clackin' louder than a loose door on a windy day.

Just as Burt opened the cash register, Matilda (who'd
gotten to the really good part of her story) boomed
from the back, "This is Sheriff Smuckley! Put yer
hands up—we've got you surrounded!"

The robbers turned white as marshmallows. Burt
tackled 'em to the floor.

Hearing the commotion, Matilda raced out front. She whipped off her hairnet and lassoed the varmints' wrists. Then she pinned them together with her name tag.

After the police hauled the robbers away, Matilda brought
Ralph Q. Yuckley a bowl of hot chili to calm his nerves.

"Thank you kindly," he said. "But I reckon what I should
be eatin' is a mighty big piece of humble pie. You two saved
my life! *And* you got this place shinin' cleaner than my
mama's kitchen." He grinned as he tore up the citations.

"But," he continued, "there's just one itty-bitty problem. That story of yours, missy . . ."

"That *story* saved your life!" Burt objected.

"And I'm not budgin' an inch till I hear the end of it. Would you tell it, Miz Matilda? *Please?*"

"Tsk, tsk, tsk," Matilda replied. "I'm afraid that's impossible—seein' as how we don't have an entertainment license."

Yuckley winked. "You do now."

The whole diner celebrated long into the night with chili, dancin', songs, and of course, Matilda's stories. It was nearly closing time when Matilda realized she hadn't seen hide nor hair of Burt in hours. No one else had, either.

Then Matilda noticed a light in the back room.

"Burt!" Matilda boomed. "What in tarnation are you doin'? You missed the whole party!"

"It was the most amazin' thing," he said. "There I was makin' chili when an idea hit me like a freight train. I figured either I'd jump on and go where it took me or just stay put and watch it pass me by. So," he continued, placing a stack of papers in Matilda's hands, "I decided to ride it."

A grin as big as Texas lit Matilda's face as she commenced to read.

"Matilda worked at Burt's Diner on the corner of Fifth and Main. But her mind was usually somewhere else: duelin' pirates, lassoin' bad guys, or wrestlin' twisters with one hand tied behind her back. . . ."

Many thanks to both my family and Michele Burke, for their ever-lovin' patience with the real Matilda. —L.D.

To my wife, Keryn, who is creative, full of ideas, and ready to "jump on and see where they take her." —T.B.

THIS IS A BORZOI BOOK PUBLISHED BY ALFRED A. KNOPF

www.randomhouse.com/kids

Educators and librarians, for a variety of teaching tools, visit us at www.randomhouse.com/teachers

Library of Congress Cataloging-in-Publication Data
Downey, Lynn.
Matilda's humdinger / by Lynn Downey ; illustrated by Tim Bowers. — 1st ed.
    p.   cm.
SUMMARY: Although Matilda the cat is the worst waitress at Burt's Diner because her mind is usually somewhere else—dueling pirates, lassoing bad guys, or wrestling twisters with one hand behind her back—no one cares since she is also the best storyteller.
ISBN 0-375-82403-0 (trade) — ISBN 0-375-92403-5 (lib. bdg.)
ISBN-13: 978-0-375-82403-6 (trade) — ISBN-13: 978-0-375-92403-3 (lib. bdg.)
[1. Storytelling—Fiction. 2. Cats—Fiction. 3. Waiters and waitresses—Fiction. 4. Diners (Restaurants)—Fiction. 5. Animals—Fiction.] I. Bowers, Tim, ill. II. Title.
PZ7.D75915Mat 2006
[Fic]—dc22
2005035822

MANUFACTURED IN CHINA
10 9 8 7 6 5 4 3 2 1
First Edition